Tom's Place

The Adventure Begins

Written and Illustrated by

Dusty Fowler

Index

Prelude

Being classed as a loner never bothered Tom. He enjoyed time alone. He felt he could only share his inner-feelings and thoughts with his one friend, Sarah. All Tom's hopes and dreams come to a halt when he discovers a hidden world beneath his feet, literally. Tom wonders to his favourite reading and time-passing spot in a nearby forest.

Things begin to change around him and within him. He stumbles on an adventure that will change his life and that of his dearest friend. Learning about the world we live in and how the simplest of things can change the lives of everyone and everything on planet Earth.

Chapter One

One thing was for certain, this was no ordinary day.

Tom was bored at home. The day seemed as though it was dragging on. He had to wait until his older brother Max got home from his day job before he was allowed to venture out. Someone had to stay at home and look after Ginger, their cat, who had been in a fight with the neighbourhood bully, a mean looking black and white cat, and so was limping around the house looking for sympathy. Mom thought it best to keep Ginger at home for at least a week.

Finally, the old clock in the kitchen made its unusual clicking sound that indicated three o'clock had arrived and Max would be home any second. He liked to be punctual, his favourite car show would start on TV in a few minutes and he got grumpy if he missed the beginning. At twelve years old, Tom was not quite a teenager yet, but taller than all the kids in his class and almost as tall as Max, who was nineteen and working already.

The slamming of the front door alerted Tom to his older brother's entrance. The TV remote rattled as Max pressed the 'on' switch and the house was filled immediately with the sounds of revving engines as Max's car show began. Tom grabbed his bag and made a run for the front door, as Max shouted "Be back at six, no later!"

When Dad wasn't around, Max was the man of the house. Tom had to obey Max's rules and he did so out of respect for his older sibling.

Tom walked across the fields separating their housing complex from nearby Granger Woods. The woods had been threatened with elimination by land developers a few years ago, but the Town Council protested in Parliament and the trees were saved. Thankfully, because Tom loved to spend as much time there as possible, right through all the seasons.

Being alone never bothered Tom. He enjoyed the forest. Sometimes, he imagined he was a Samurai, chopping heads off of flowers with a stick, pretending they were unworthy peasants or dangerous enemies.

Other days, he made believe he was a soldier, crawling through the undergrowth and sniping at passers-by, usually pensioners out walking their dogs.

He decided he would make his way past the old mill today. It was just an empty shell of a building now, but Dad said it had been a mill many years ago. Funny, Tom was convinced he could still smell bread here in the summer. Walking at a casual pace, he skirted the dam, sometimes skimming stones over the surface and made his way to his favourite tree.

A big old oak stood on the edge of the dam. This is where Tom loved to spend many hours on his own. At the base of the tree, which had been struck by lightning, a huge arch-shaped hole had been formed that went deep into the tree, a perfect hiding place for a young boy to crawl into. He was at peace here. No annoying older brother and very few people ever came this far into the woods. Tom could sit there for hours and watch whatever happened around him. There was an old fox hunting for mice in the long grass. The fox's keen nose could smell Tom, but as long as he sat perfectly still, Tom knew the fox would ignore him and carry on searching for food.

Chapter Two

Looking at his watch, Tom realised he had been gone for an hour already. Time really did fly when you weren't paying attention to it. So why did it not go even half as fast when you needed it to? On his hands and knees, Tom crawled through the tree's archway and deep into the tree. It was very quiet. There seemed to be just an owl for company today.

Most of the old brown oak leaves had fallen and the new, light green buds and leaves were showing all over the tree's huge branches. Summer was on its way. Tom turned to face the entrance of his hide-away, while he sat with his back leaning against the inside wall of the tree. It hadn't been burnt this far back, but it still smelled of charcoal and barbeques. No bugs seemed to bother him here. He had also never seen any droppings left by other creatures in here. Looking out from his safe place, he could see far beyond the top of the long grass, a few red and yellow flowers dotted randomly at the forest edge.

Tom's Archway

Sitting with his legs tucked away under him gave him cramps, so he got up and sat on his bag, forgetting that he had put his sandwiches and a banana in there earlier this morning.

As he leaned back to enjoy his few hours of solitude, he suddenly heard a strange click and a whooshing sound, and before he could react, he was sliding backwards and downwards. In total panic, he tried to turn around, or to hold onto something at the same time, which just seemed to make him slide faster downwards.

The walls around him were now black, like polished stone, there was nothing to hold onto. With a sense of dread, he slid downwards at a forty-five-degree angle. He kept falling and trying to slow himself down by grabbing at the walls, but they were as smooth as glass. Tom thought he was never going to get out of there again and he would definitely never make it back for Max's six o clock curfew.

However, suddenly he landed with a bump. He had scraped his shin-bone on an outcrop of roots at the base of the long dark slide. He winced when he saw that blood ran into his sock.

For a minute or two, Tom sat on his bottom and tried to get a good look around. He was in some kind of chamber.

Light was coming from up ahead, so he crawled in that direction. To his amazement, he could feel soft velvet-like material just in front of him. The light was shining through a tiny gap from underneath something that looked like drapes.

Chapter Three

Not sure where he was or what he was doing, Tom pressed his left eye to the hole in the curtain and almost fell backwards, giving off a shriek.

A deep voice on the other side said, "Sir, we have an unexpected visitor!" And with that, a clawed hand whipped the curtain to one side, revealing a room filled with books, very small books and two very strange looking creatures.

The taller one had the face of an old tawny owl, but hands and feet similar to our own, while the shorter creature had the head of a rat, clawed hands and the six-limbed body of an ant.

Now inside the room, Tom found himself surrounded by the tiny books. The owl thing was human shaped, but with an owl's head and a human mouth. Its wings ended in small hands with three fingers instead of four and a long thumb.

Turning to his right, Tom saw the scary ant-like creature with its six ant-like limbs. And if you think such strange appearances would mean that these creatures would be evil, then think again. One should never judge a book by its cover because Tom and this creature would become very good friends.

However, right now, Tom just stood there in shock and turned to try and run away. The owl-thing said to him, 'The way you came in is a lift that has now departed. You can only enter or leave once the moon has risen!" Tom got upset and said, "But Sir, my brother will be very angry, if I'm not home by six o'clock!" The owl-thing replied, "We don't understand your o'clocks, but we can take you to someone who does!" Tom choked back his fear, forgot his manners and called out, "Who and what are you?" The rat-thing said, "We'll have time for explanations later, but now it's time to eat, follow us."

Glancing backwards at the curtain and the possible escape route, Tom tried to swallow a dry mouthful of fear and followed these two strange creatures up a darkened corridor, which reminded Tom of the time he had been trying to look down a foxhole in the forest.

A sort of shuffling sound in front of the trio brought them to a halt, as a huge worm-like creature the size of Tom's Dad's car shuffled past. It had no eyes, but two huge mandibles sniffing and feeling its way forward. Tom could almost see through it, the faint pink skin was so thin and dry looking, a mere membrane of tissue separated Tom from nasty, creepy, moving organs. The rat-thing turned and stared at Tom. It then said in a tight whisper, "When you hear the shuffle, never move, never ever move, those slugs can hear your heart beat and they eat anything. These tunnels around us are all made by the slugs." Tom tried to peer down the

tunnel to see the shuffling slug, but all he could see

was the wiggling rear end of the huge worm-like

'slug'.

Chapter Four

As the three moved forward in the tunnel, a barking sound could be heard off to the left. Tom froze as though ice was seeping through his veins. Rat-thing and owl–thing turned suddenly and stared at him. He could only squeak, "What? What's wrong?" The owl-thing leaned closer and sniffed and what seemed to Tom like a hungry smile went across the owl–things face, as he looked up. Tom could see the smile never reached its eyes, when it said, "We can smell your fear, it excites us and the dogs up there in your world can also smell it. It drives them into a frenzy and that makes them dig holes. That means we then have to sacrifice a prisoner, to keep our secrets hidden."

Tom gulped again and swore to himself that wherever he was, he would do his upmost to control or conceal his fears in the future. He didn't want to be exciting any creature that could smell his fear.

The dining hall that Tom was taken into was like nothing he had ever seen before. Tom stood with his mouth wide open, staring at the darkened room. He could notice lots of movement, but the light wasn't bright enough to see what was moving. The owl-thing held out its hand and screeched a very high-pitched yell that sounded to Tom's ears like "EEEEEEYYYYAAAWWWW!'

All movement stopped. Then a deep voice growled, "Who dares disturb dinner?" Owl-thing replied, "I do, Master Owl, Bookery!" Then the rat-thing called out, "Lights, please!" A few seconds passed and then bright lights shone down from the ceiling and from the sides of the walls.

Tom, who had only recently closed his mouth again, found that it was hanging open once more. Around him were creatures he didn't recognise. Fusions of animals he knew, mixed and blended with animals, insects and what appeared to be fish and crabs. They sat or crawled in rows of concentric circles, eating fruit and drinking from old jam jars. There were no plates and no cutlery, but one creature had what appeared to be a knife at the end of its wrist, where Tom had a hand.

An owl-like creature with the body of a lion leapt in front of Tom and said, "Human, you're not welcome here!" The owl-thing quickly stepped between Tom and the owl-lion and said, "All creatures are welcome here, except if they break the rules. Nobody but Uncle can decide." With that the owl-lion creature stepped back and beckoned Tom to join the feast.

Tom sat with his two companions either side of him. An ant the size of a dog, but with a long face and huge eyes, gave Tom figs wrapped in a lettuce leaf and instructed simply, "Eat."

The noise returned to the room, the slurping and crunching of many creatures eating. Tom ate a little of the fig and tried not to stare at all these extraordinary sights around him. The lights dimmed again, but not the same kind of darkness as before. Maybe his eyes were getting used to this. He tried his friendly smile on one toad-looking creature and got a toothless smile in return. The toad hopped over and spoke in a strange squeaky voice.

"Why you here?" Without waiting for an answer, the toad turned to Tom's owl thing companion and said, "Eeyaaw. Why bring human here?" Owl-thing and toad locked themselves in a high-pitched conversation that Tom could not follow. As he looked around the room, Tom realised that most of the creatures were looking straight at him. Some were licking their lips as if he was on their menu and others giving him that cold lifeless stare of someone who didn't care. The rat-thing said, "Don't make eye contact. It's considered unfriendly from strangers." Tom was starting to get a feel for this strange world, referred to by its residents as 'Down'. Depending on just how deep down you were living, there seemed to be a system and an order. Some of the creatures were friendly, others were clearly not.

Chapter Five

A clawed hand gripped Tom on his forearm and snapped him out of his deep thoughts. Rat-thing said, "Excuse us, we haven't introduced ourselves. I'm Melk. This wise old trakker here is Trendor. He doesn't say a lot, except if it's absolutely necessary." Tom glanced to his left and saw Trendor was stuffing handfuls of worms and fennel leaves into his human-like mouth. "We are the Bookers." Melk explained to Tom that every creature ever born or hatched in 'Up' or 'Down' was recorded by the Bookers. Their whole lifespan was recorded in tiny books. "That includes you, your brother and your whole family."

Melk the Crendle

Tom got up and asked, "Are you guys like God?"

Melk answered, "Your God doesn't do all the work

on his own. He would never get everything done.

We are his Dookers, we are directed by Uncle. We

will introduce him to you and you to him if he joins

us for feeding today," Melk explained to Tom.

The barking that was echoing through the hall faded away, to be replaced by an almost audible silence. Then the whispering began and Tom could hear one word repeated over and over by every creature in the room, until it became a chant. "Uncle", "Uncle", "Uncle", "Uncle", "Uncle", "UNCLE", "UNCLE!"

An owl the size of a fridge walked into the hall, raised its wings and called out "EEYAAWW!" Tom had learned from Melk that this was their greeting, similar to our 'Hello'. Behind the owl stood a huge woman in a gown that looked like it had been woven from leaves, twigs and what looked like faces of a million different creatures carved out of tiny pieces of wood. She stepped into the light at the centre of the room and Tom realised that the tiny carved wooden faces all over her dress were actually talking in soft voices. From his distance, Tom couldn't hear what they were saying, he could only see their lips moving. Behind her stood an enormous man. He was old, but he looked strong and powerful. He greeted everyone with a beady eye, and although he was talking to the whole room, he looked you straight in the eye and made each word he spoke feel as though it was spoken for you alone. Something struck Tom instantly. These people were very tall and unusually wide and muscular, in a way that reminded him of body builders at his father's gym.

Tom looked around, all the faces of hundreds of strange, yet beautiful creatures were staring up at 'Uncle'. The ant-like creature appeared at Tom's side and escorted him away from his companions. Melk said, "Just go, you'll be safe, enjoy." So, with a backward glance at his new-found companions, Tom was escorted towards the front, where the man called 'Uncle' was. The owl and the lady were in deep conversation, when ants with rat faces pushed Tom past a multitude of strange, but somehow familiar creatures. He was herded like a sheep, gently but firmly nudged and shoved along from both sides and the back, until he was standing in front of the huge man.

Staring at the man, Tom could see movement beneath the skin, the blood seemed to be alive, as if it had a life of its own. It occasionally rippled the skin as it moved along with quite some force. Standing there with his arms aloft, the man commanded silence in the room. He threw a stern glance at the gossiping woman and the enormous owl.

Then this huge man spoke. The room trembled at the sound of his booming voice. "A human has broken our sacred code! What must we do with him?"

It was a rhetorical question. Tom could see excitement in the creatures' faces around him. He was convinced now that he would be eaten. The man turned to look at Tom and shouted, "Age?" Tom stood dumbfounded. He was about to answer, when the man turned to Melk and Trendor and exclaimed, "Your human, does it speak?" Trendor answered, "Yes, Uncle, it has thought!" The man turned back towards the crowd and said, "We have a prisoner and we also have a guest."

"Only the human's thought can guide us and show us what decision we should make." With that, the man leaned forward and clasped his huge hands on either side of Tom's head and lifted him clear off the floor. It was a little uncomfortable to be held

like that, but Tom was assured by the memory of

Melk's words, when he had told Tom to 'enjoy'.

Chapter Six

A low humming rose in Tom's ears, then a cold blue light filled his mind and he saw images run in front of his mind's eye as if a tiny projector was playing a movie there. At first, Tom didn't recognise the young child in the moving pictures, but then he saw pictures of his parents. Tom suddenly realised he was watching footage of his own life to date.

Tom saw an older teen of himself grow into a young soldier, then later as a vet, transforming into a father of three children: a girl and two boys. He saw a beautiful marriage on a beach somewhere hot; he saw smiling faces of politicians as he was awarded some certificate. He then saw an elderly couple sitting on a park bench.

Finally, he watched an old woman in a hospital bed, with the man holding her hand and crying. Tom realised at that point that he was witnessing scenes illustrating his own life. It was all planned and mapped out before him. This made him wonder, if any of his decisions were his own or predetermined by a higher authority? The cold blue light slowly faded in his mind. He felt how his feet met the floor under him again.

The huge man's hands released Tom and the man spoke in his deep loud voice. "The human is pure of heart. His soul is young; he hasn't enough experience in the 'Up' yet to understand evil. This prisoner is now our guest and will be treated with the upmost respect. You will all help and guide him as long as it takes." The man then turned, looked at Tom and said, "We are your servants. We are sorry that you are upon us, but we are excited and a little frightened of your presence.

"Humans live in the 'Up' and not here. Our codes forbid mixing with humans, but we now know your intentions are pure. You mean us no harm." The man looked at Tom for a few quiet seconds and then said, "Your o'clock has stopped up there. From the moment you slipped through the hatch of the lift, everything in your world has stopped.

"Don't worry about being home for six o'clock, you will still make it. It's as though your life up there has been paused. You are in no danger. However, had we discovered cruel intentions in your heart or your mind, you would have been eaten, and therefore recycled back into the system. So, enjoy your time here. Use it wisely and learn how the world really works.

There is 'Up,' you are proof of that and there is 'Down,' as you have found. Look around, these creatures are all real. What you see are animals, fish and birds entwined in lives so complex that grasping the thought for just a second will send your mind into a spin, which you will not recover from. Look here, these are Crendles. The ant-rat like creatures are our servants but also our soldiers. The knife-like blade at the end of their front limbs is used to carry food and other items but they can be turned very swiftly into blades for war.

These Crendles in the hall are youngsters, in your time scale, they would be less than a year old. They serve and guard every creature. When they reach their second year, they are too big for this hall and are driven away to form their own colonies elsewhere in the deep 'Down.'

"Melk is a hybrid of the cunning Rat and a Crendle. His mind is quick, but his six-limbed body of a Crendle is quicker. Trendor was once a human, just like you. His gambling got him into trouble and he was buried alive in the desert. I rescued him myself. An owl is a symbol for wisdom in your world, so I gave Trendor the features of an owl. His body is still human, but it regenerates every six full moons, so he will never grow old. Other owls love and respect Trendor because they would so love to be just a little bit human, whereas he has ninety percent of the package. There are many other creatures here that you may or may not recognise. Most are hybrids to serve a purpose down here. We keep them hidden from the 'Up' as they would be taken away and experimented on, which only ends in their death. The Stank are our prison guards. They decide, which creature may be hunted by your dogs. When a dog catches a rabbit or a bird, have you ever wondered why the creature is always dead? That's so that we keep our secrets. To transform one of us to our original state always ends with death." "Any questions?"

Chapter Seven

Tom didn't know where to begin, so he thought to just play it by ear. He introduced himself, but refrained from telling the man anything about himself as he was sure the man knew more than he let on. The man, Tom was sure, must be God. He just knew so much about everything, and every creature seemed to work for him in one way or another.

Tom felt as though everything was a test. He wanted to ask questions about everything: the creatures, the food, the power source, everything. The man stood and told him, "Follow me." Tom was guided up a dark corridor. As they walked down the passageway, Tom could see windows made from crystallised glass that seemed to be in parts honeycombed like in a beehive and in other parts shimmering like the scales on a fish.

Behind these crystal windows, Tom could see all kinds of processes taking place, ranging from chemistry and maths in classrooms to food being washed and prepared. Uncle stopped before a large wooden door with a tiny circular window in its centre, looked at Tom and said, "Within this room, you may make no sounds, do you understand?" Tom nodded.

Uncle called out in a loud voice, "Open" and the door slid upwards in a smooth soundless motion. Uncle walked into the room and beckoned for Tom to follow. All around, the earth-covered walls were tiny ant-like movements. Only on closer inspection, could Tom see tiny people, going about their daily lives, in a tiny world.

As Tom looked even closer, he could see small cars, buses and trains all interwoven within the earth walls. there was no up or down, no east or west; everything and everyone was churning and writhing around like snakes in a basket.

Tom walked up to a part of the mass and could see a tiny version of his own house. Following the images to the left, he could see a tiny ant-sized young man curled up on the tiny doll's-house-sized sofa and he realised he was looking at his brother, Max.

Tom thought this was probably the most extraordinary thing he had ever seen. He could follow his own path, with different images of himself at home and then in the woods. Wow, everything was here! Wondering what would happen next, Tom tried to follow the ant-sized people up the wall to the next image, but found it difficult to focus. Around some of the older looking people and animals were ghost-like and similar, but see through images. Tom tried to remind himself of all the questions he had, which were building up in his mind.

As he turned to look at Uncle, the door through which they had come in, opened and Trendor stood there, staring at the floor. Uncle went to him and they both went out. Tom looked around the room, there was movement everywhere. The walls, ceiling and floor were all moving. Tiny creatures were looking after everything, they were guiding ant-sized people through their everyday lives. One thing that stood out amongst all the movement was that Max was unmoving and a tiny figure of Tom still lay asleep in the burnt-out arch of the big old oak tree.

He turned and walked to the wooden door. Peering through the small glass window, he saw the eyeballs and eyebrows of Uncle and Trendor. The door opened silently again and Uncle grabbed Tom's arm and pulled him back into the corridor, as the door slid down shut behind him.

Uncle explained that everyone and everything that breathed air was in that room. The fish were elsewhere, but as Tom wasn't related to a fish – as far as he knew, it wasn't important for him to see their lives. This sort of, somehow, made sense. Tom almost laughed out loud; in this crazy world, he had found something that almost made sense!

Uncle explained how the Crendles were willing servants, but they played the role of an army if the need ever arose. The Bookers were all creatures, blended and hybrids all working together.

Melk, Uncle and Trendor sat beside Tom on long benches along the edge of one corridor. The benches had no legs and seemed just to be part of the wall, woven around roots and pieces of branches of hundreds of different types of wood.

Trendor spoke first. He told Tom that everyone had work to do here; all creatures ranging from the smallest fly to the huge slugs clearing the passage ways and that just because time had stopped in his

'Up', down here, life carried on and they needed to get back to work.

Corridor Slug

A CORRIDOR SLUG

Tom was free to roam around and explore for himself, but was warned that if he had no purpose to be in a room, then the door would simply not open; and if he didn't want to be recycled or eaten, he must at all costs be aware of the slugs cleaning the passageways. Melk held onto Tom's hand and squeezed and shook at the same time. He didn't say a word, just got up and followed Trendor.

Who could imagine that a creature such as Melk could even exist? He had a scary rat's face, was as big as a horse and had six legs sticking out of his wasp- or ant-like body. The foreleg ending in a blade was fearsome, but Melk was charming and friendly.

That left Tom alone again with Uncle. Uncle looked lost in deep thought, so Tom just sat quietly and waited for Uncle to say something. Finally, Uncle turned to Tom after what seemed to Tom like ten minutes and said, "Similar to your world, here also some things are very dangerous. Creatures here would eat you if they thought they could get away with it, but I am in control here. I work directly as a servant to God. The lady you saw in the eating hall is Mother Nature.

She is my wife and lifelong companion. All the creatures here are God's creations, but he leaves it to me to change kindred souls of two infinitely different creatures to create one sustainable soul. How you live your life in the 'Up', will determine if you belong there or here. It's not your choice, but rather the choices you make. Do you see?

Tom sat back on the bench for a moment and thought about all he had been told and all that he had seen. He was about to ask Uncle a question, when the corridor went suddenly dark and the bench Tom had been sitting on slid backwards into the wall, almost throwing Tom to the floor.

Uncle tapped his hands on the floor and a ring of light glowed around each of his wrists, like bracelets made completely out of light. Tom could see a slug only two metres away, shuffling its way towards them. He could see its front that meant business was nowhere near as cute as the rear. Directly in the centre of this strange creature was a churning, grinding mouth, with teeth moving in a slow circular motion that picked up and twisted anything that got in its path.

A door opened and a Crendle came out. It looked to its left at Tom and Uncle, but before either of them could shout a warning, it was drawn backwards into the large mouth, six legs snapping like twigs, folding in on themselves as they twisted. Then the head and body were next, crushed in a heartbeat. Uncle grabbed Tom's hand and dragged him up the corridor and away from the very hungry mouth of the slug. He pushed Tom through a doorway and waved his arms in circles until the lights at his wrists faded. He said, "Here, young man, you have to be quick; hesitation will get you recycled or dead." "I must go now, many things here need my attention.

Enjoy your exploring, we will see each other again

soon."

Chapter Eight

Tom walked slowly up the corridor, not wanting to get in the way of any slugs and be recycled like that poor Crendle. On his immediate right, he found a door made from old milk bottles. He could see movement inside the room, but couldn't see exactly what was happening, so he took a deep breath, calmed himself and stood in front of the door and said 'Open.' The door swung inwards.

Crendles were working around an animal that looked to Tom as if it was a moose. Tom had seen a photo of one, from an old scrapbook when his Father had travelled to Canada. Walking down its furry flank, Tom could see the Crendles crawling all over the moose like ants. They seemed to be cleaning it. A Crendle stepped forward and said to Tom, 'I saw you at our feeding hall. Did Melk explain how we can shift body size to change our needs? Well, we have lots of work to do on this old moose and if we were all your size, the moose and this chamber would be overcrowded quickly. So, we shrink down individually or as a team."

Cleaning the Moose

Tom started to understand a bit better, but these things were all new to him and unexpected. Almost like a car wash, but in complete silence, the Crendles worked up and down, around and around.

When Tom reached the moose's face, he saw two huge brown eyes staring unblinkingly at the wall in front. Tom asked, "What's wrong with him?" The nearest Crendle turned to Tom and explained that when an animal gets too old to look after itself, it is brought down here and cleaned up and fed before being returned to the 'Up'; then, when it's really old, it will either be recycled or reused elsewhere.

Nothing really dies completely. Tom stood fascinated, wondering if this would happen to him when he was old and frail. Like Granddad. Oh my word, would Granddad be hoovered and fed like the old moose? He laughed to himself as he thought of his Granddad swearing and cursing as millions of little creatures worked all over him.

Then, without addressing anyone in particular, Tom asked, "How does it work then? Do you stop his 'o'clock too then?" From down at Tom's feet he heard a little voice say, "Almost, animals don't stick to the same time-scale as humans do, but they do have a purpose. This moose that you are so worried about is actually a mother to lots of little moose and we should be getting her back soon for feeding time, so please move along and entertain yourself elsewhere."

With that, two Crendles opened their blade-like hands outwards and moved towards Tom in a threatening manner. He got the message and headed for the door. Another Crendle stopped him and said, "You can never leave by the door you came in." Tom hastily looked around, but could see no other door. He closed his eyes, calmed his beating heart and said rather loudly 'OPEN!' A door appeared open right in front of him and he gladly stepped through it. He wasn't back out in the corridor as he had hoped, but in another room.

Cold steel looking aluminium shelves with jars stacked floor to ceiling ran as far as Tom could see. The jars were filled with a clear liquid and objects that Tom hoped he would never see in a jar. Human eyeballs, one marked brown, another marked blue, and so on. Ears of all different shapes and sizes.

Eyebrows and eyelashes. Noses and hair. Short hair and long hair, everything seemed to be kept in jars. Tom was just starting to get freaked out, when a mouth in one of the jars started to laugh in a strange underwater type laugh. Tom moved on. In clear crystal cases, Tom saw arms, legs and feet. Then antlers and claws. He got to the end of the room with his breath held between clenched teeth and could barely squeak the word "Open." A door

behind him swung inwards, nearly knocking him off

his feet. He spun around and was relieved to find

himself back in the corridor once again.

Chapter Nine

As Tom walked carefully up and down the corridors, he began to realise that everything that was supposed to happen naturally up in his world was actually controlled from down here. Rotations of the earth around the sun seemed natural to Tom but if you think about the timing of just about everything, it's far too well organised for humans. Sixty seconds to a minute, sixty minutes to an hour and twenty-four hours in a day. No room for mistakes. Cutting it fine, to say the least.

Tom stopped in front of a door marked as Memories. He looked around at a darkened room with nothing except a single wooden stool in its centre. The only source of light was about a hundred fire flies chasing each other in the roof panels. He pulled the stool over to a curved wall, sat and leaned his aching back against the strangely warm wall and closed his eyes.

Click. Clang! Thud! Whoosh! Tom's chair was moving! The chair had thrown a harness twice around Tom's waist, then up his back and over both shoulders, pinning his bottom into the seat of the stool. Tom held onto the front of the stool with one hand and gripped his bag in the other hand. He was scared, but was also enjoying the ride. The chair had started to move quite smoothly. Not like a horse, but more like a skateboard. It wasn't rolling, it was running.

The door opened outwards like a garage door as Tom approached, clinging to the stool. It turned immediately to its left and ran at a high speed down the first corridor. It braked suddenly and skirted around a group of Crendles carrying food down the corridor. It ran so fast that Tom could only grin at passers-by instead of the usual waved greeting. It ran and ran, up one corridor and down the next, not always staying in the middle of the floor as we would walk, but occasionally running up the walls and along the ceiling.

The chair ran through an open clearing, where trees grew. A stream trickled down over rocks and fairies fluttered like butterflies all around. Tom had to cover his eyes as it seemed the rays of sun shining through the leafy canopy would make his eyeballs explode in his head. He blinked back tears and once again the chair was speeding down another corridor.

They screeched to a halt outside an enormous wooden door. The buckles and straps holding Tom in place, loosened and the chair tipped forward, depositing Tom into a half crouched, half seated position. The chair sped off, leaving Tom bewildered. He was about to knock on the door, when it split straight down its centre and both sides swung inwards. Crendles took up one side of the room. They seemed to be shifting through rocks, looking for something.

A long wooden table stretched out before Tom. Creatures stood on differently sized chairs down both sides of the table. Some creatures were reading, some were painting, while others read books or typed on the old-style typewriters. Each of the Crendles had a number of fairies assisting them with whatever they seemed to be doing. As Tom approached the nearest Crendle, it turned its rat-like face towards him, grinned and then stepped one pace to its right, leaving a gap for Tom.

The Creative Room

Tom dutifully filled the gap. Quickly, a group of three fairies came up to Tom and squeaked and pointed at him. He was unsure of what they meant, so he touched his chest and said, "Tom." They looked at each other and giggled, which sounded like tiny tubular bells.

The fairy on the right parroted, "Dohm!" The other two started singing 'Dohm', over and over again. Tom stepped just slightly forward and said in a clear crisp voice "Tom", not 'Dohm!' "Tom!", as in Tomato. The fairies looked at each other again, then burst into more giggles. A loud clapping sound stopped the fun. Every creature in the room stopped what they were doing and bowed towards the door behind Tom. It took Tom a second or two to realise that he wasn't bowing and was facing the wrong way. The Crendle nearest him reached out with four of its strange three-fingered hands and turned Tom towards the door.

Tom stared at the floor. A leafy, earthy smell filled his nostrils, followed by the scents of flowers and honey. Tom looked up and his jaw dropped open.

Chapter Ten

Mother Nature stood before all the creatures. She wore a woven gown of fine cotton and leather strands. Around her waist was a belt of pure gold. On each wrist was a bracelet of silver. She clapped her hands and all the creatures turned and continued what they were doing before. Except Tom. He stood staring at the wonder and beauty of this woman before him. Since losing his grandmother to a long cancer battle, he had had no contact with women other than his Geography teacher. The lady walked past Tom and said simply, "Follow." Tom walked behind her as they walked the length of the table, where the creatures were going about their business.

A circle of light appeared on the floor in front of them and as they got closer, it widened enough for just the two of them to stand in it. The light grew up the sides, then all around, until the two of them were standing in what appeared to be a tube of light. Then Tom heard a clicking and whooshing sound and the floor beneath them gave way and it felt as if they both travelled straight up.

There was nothing under Tom's feet, no floor just darkness.

Whoosh, the wind brushed past Tom's ears at great speed, but it wasn't cold or frightening. They began to slow down, then came to a stop in a field full of dairy cows. Tom recognised this as the meadow near his school.

Mother Nature told Tom to stand perfectly still. She then told Tom to walk towards one of the cows, which he did. There was a bright flash of light behind him and when he turned, she was gone.

He stood alone in the field for quite a while, wondering what had just happened. He was back in his own time and space. He turned and walked back towards the tree line. He was less than half a kilometre from the old oak tree.

He slung his bag over his shoulder and ran as fast as he could. He got to the tree, half expecting to see himself still sitting there, but the arch-way was empty except for a few twigs and leaves.

Why did they let him return now? There were so many unanswered questions. He was unsure what to do next. He walked through the woods back to his house. He reached the garden gate and sneaked into the kitchen through the back door.

He was just getting himself a glass of milk, when his brother Max appeared from the living room, swiped Tom across the head and said, "I thought you were going out?" Tom looked at his watch and realised that only two hours had passed since Max had warned him to be back on time.

Tom said he'd changed his mind and would be going to his room instead. He asked Max if he could use the house phone, to which his brother answered, "Probably to phone that little chick of yours. Ok, but make it quick." Tom frowned, he didn't like his best friend Sarah to be referred to as a chick and normally, he would have said something back, but right now he desperately felt he had to speak to someone about all he'd seen and heard, otherwise he thought he would burst.

Chapter Eleven

"Hello?" Sarah's mother asked almost immediately on the other end of the telephone line. "Oh hello, Mrs Davidson, it's Thomas Sincock here. Could I speak to Sarah, please?" Then he heard her call, "Sarah, it's the Sincock boy on the line for you..." and a clunk, as the house phone receiver was placed hard on the wooden table.

Tom heard a muffled cough and then Sarah's sweet voice, "Hi, Thomas." Tom answered, "Sarah, hi. I need to see you as soon as possible, something strange and unusual has happened. Can you come over, please? "Sarah said she first needed to get ready and she would wait at his back garden gate in half an hour. Tom walked into the living room and sat quietly until an advertisement break allowed him to speak to his older brother.

"Max, Sarah's coming over and then we are going for a walk. I have sarmies and a Snicker with me, so won't be back for 18:00, ok?" Max just looked at Tom with a sideward smile and replied, "Whatever!"

Tom unpacked the old cellophane covered sandwich he still had in the bottom of his bag, dumped it in the bin and replaced it with some fresh sandwiches from the fridge. He then took two Snickers from the cupboard, with the plan of giving one to Sarah. He added two soft drinks from the fridge.

He sat on his grandfather's saggy old reading chair and thought about how and what he would tell Sarah.

She was his best friend and he had never lied to her before, but this was different, this story was weird. Would she believe such a strange and unusual story, even if it was all true? He had to try and see if she would believe him. He saw Sarah's blonde hair shimmering in the sunlight, so he stepped through the French window style doors with their ghastly floral pattern curtains and up the garden path to meet her.

"So, Monsieur Sincock, what's so important that you had to drag me away from a day at the mall?" Tom asked her if she would just walk with him to his secret place. He had told her that he had a special place to go and sit, read and think, but he had never taken anyone there before.

They walked in silence to the edge of the forest, then followed an old deer trail in single file until they reached the small meadow, where Tom's big old oak stood at the furthest edge. From this angle, you couldn't see the burnt-out archway.

Sarah stopped and called out, "Wow, Tom! This is a beautiful thinking spot." He grinned and took her hand and led her towards the old oak. "This is where it all started." She looked down and could see at the base of the tree an arch burnt into the trunk as though the tree had been struck by lightning.

From where she was standing in the long grass, she could just see the right edge of the arch. She moved around to the front and got down on her knees.

Brushing a few dead leaves and twigs out of the way, she sat down. Looking into the arch, she couldn't see all the way to the back. "Go right in," said Tom. Without looking back or hesitating, she crawled forward using her hands and gently swinging her bottom forwards until she sat with her feet touching the rear curved wall of the huge old oak's inner trunk.

She felt Tom's breath on her neck as he said, "Close your eyes and count to twenty, then your eyes will adjust to the darkness." He sat beside her and told her to turn around so that they both faced the entrance. He explained that he came here to sit and think and watch the world go by. He told her that in the summer, it was nice and cool here, where he could sit unbothered by midges and ants. In the winter, it was warm and dry, where he could sit unaffected by the snowy cold landscape.

Part of the Forest

Chapter Twelve

She said, "This is all fascinating, Tom and I'm honoured that you brought me here to share your special place, but for the life of me, I can't understand why you're showing me this." He told her to just wait. So they waited. He handed her a sandwich, a Snicker bar and a coke and they sat in relative silence. Tom ate quickly, he had much to tell Sarah, but first he wanted to secure her secrecy.

"Promise me that you won't tell a single soul about what it is I am about to share with you."

She rolled her eyes, stuffed in the last bite of her Snicker bar, held out her hand and said, "I promise." A split second later, there was an audible click, the floor beneath their bottoms slipped away and the two of them began sliding downwards and backwards. Sarah shrieked and grabbed Tom's thigh.

He put his arm around her and said, "Don't be scared, this will change your life." As before, when Tom had been on his own, they were dumped unceremoniously on the floor of the curtained room.

Tom said to Sarah, "Just give it a minute for your eyes to adjust to the dark." Sarah felt her heart beating loudly in her chest and she turned to Tom and whispered, "This had better be worth it!" A clawed hand reached around the edge of the curtain and whipped it aside. Sarah screeched and backed into Tom. Tom said, "It's okay. He's friendly." And their journey began.

Back in our world, Tom's brother sat and watched Top Gear. Jeremy Clarkson was racing an Audi RS4 up a mountainside in the Alps, while a couple of freeclimbers did their best to beat him to the top. Time had slowed just slightly, but no one except those brain boxes would have noticed. Tom's brother would not be at all surprised that his annoying little brother and his female companion had everything to do with the Earth's spin slowing for one hundredth of a second.

"Master Sincock!" The loud voice rattled deeply through the walls around Tom and Sarah. Every creature knew the voice's owner and Tom looked at Sarah with a worried look and said, "I might be in a bit of trouble for bringing you here, but we'll just have to see, okay?" As soon as Tom had said the word 'trouble', Trendor pulled back the curtain and looked at Tom and then Sarah with his huge owl eyes. "Master Sincock, your impromptu arrival and the fact that you have returned with a human has caused alarm amongst the burrows.

"A meeting has been called, there will now be a trial." A door opened to Tom's left and two bar stools came in at a high speed. Tom turned to Sarah to explain what the chairs could do, but the chairs were followed by a platoon of angry looking Crendles that forced him and Sarah back into the seats on the stools, then stood back as the buckles fastened themselves around the two frightened children. With a blur of motion, the stools sped towards the nearest wall, not the door they had come in, but a solid wall.

With a neck-wrenching jerk, the stools went straight up the wall and out through a trap door that doubled as a skylight. Tom pulled his head as far to his right as he could and caught a flash of Sarah strapped to her stool, her hair streaming in the wind as she raced up and down corridors, on ceilings, over grass and ice and back into another corridor right beside him. He caught the sweet scent of apples and felt the bitter cold pinch his cheeks as he passed different elements and seasons in the blink of an eye.

The Crendle army kept pace and maintained an exact measurement of distance behind the high-speed stools at all times.

They burst through a bush, twigs and leaves scratching their faces and into a clearing in a forest. The ground was covered in pine needles and as Tom's eyes adjusted to the harsh sunlight filtering through the tree canopy above, he could see they were heading towards a natural-looking amphitheatre tucked into a forest. Hundreds of animals that Tom recognised were all standing in ranks according to height, facing a small clearing in the middle. As the stools sped forwards without slowing down, the animals stepped aside and then swiftly refilled the gap with the precision of trained soldiers. The stools only came to a halt in front of the lady figure Tom had seen on his previous visit.

She stood there like an angry parent with her hands on her hips and glared at Tom and Sarah with her dark brown eyes. Her magnificent gown came alive. The millions of rows of faces moved independently of each other, through a myriad of emotions. Tom looked up and could see the antlers of a huge deer;

he looked down and saw this mighty and proud beast was staring unblinkingly and straight at him.

He moved his eyes to the left, where a pair of sea eagles was perched on a branch and their eyes were staring at him, too. He knew then that every creature in this amphitheatre was drawn to him, but not by their own choice. They looked hypnotised. Mother Nature in her fabulous clothing made up from miniature faces of the people she cared for – not her family members, but the people who took care of the land in her name – ranging from doctors to presidents, from children to the elderly, she stepped forward with her hands on her hips and glared at Tom and Sarah.

"Young humans, you are on trial today." "All the creatures of the Earth, from Up and Down have sent representatives here to guide you and calm you through this process. You will not be harmed, but your fate is in your hearts and your intentions. Tom, you saw some of what we are about and were sworn not to tell a soul. You, young lady, what is your name?"

"Sarah Davidson." "I sensed hesitation, when you stated your name. Why is that?" "My mother remarried, so my last name has changed." "An acceptable reason. We will continue. By all the creatures gathered here today, we have a trial!"

Animals all around stamped their hooves and snorted loudly, building to a crescendo before calming and falling to a whisper. Tom and Sarah were still strapped to the stools that had brought them here. Sitting higher than a bar stool, they were at eye level with lots of the bigger woodland creatures. All around, animals of every kind shuffled to get a better look at the two children who would be on trial. "Silence! Who amongst us are the spirit guides for Thomas Sincock and Sarah Davidson?"

A roar came from deep in the forest. A bright blue light shone around the animal coming forward. It could be seen clearly from two hundred metres away. As it got closer, other creatures stepped aside to let the ball of light through. In the centre of the bright blue light stood an enormous Grizzly bear. It reared up onto its back legs and gave out another almighty roar, then went back down onto all fours and stood behind Tom.

Golden Eyes, the deer

A hunting horn could be heard from far off. A cracking of branches and then, as if out of nowhere, a mighty forest deer with a rack of antlers glistening in the sunlight, stood proudly in a circle of green light for just a second, so everyone could admire him, before trotting over and standing behind Sarah.

The deer and the bear switched places briefly before finally settling behind the kids again, the deer behind Sarah and the bear behind Tom. Mother Nature was amused at the sight of these two powerful spirit guides. "My, My!" she said. "Although you are just teenagers, the world has provided you with two powerful spirit guides, the brown bear and the stag. Listen to them. They will guide you through your trial. They do not know human minds, so be very careful what you choose to say and do."

With a crackling of branches and twigs, many lights started to appear through the forest as more spirit guides arrived. Tom saw a whale, an elephant, a fox and an eagle all line up behind Mother Nature in their globes of light. All different colours, shining brightly.

Creatures of the forest made way for animals from Africa. An enormous giraffe curled into a kneeling position next to guinea fowl, lions and meercats. From Asia, there were tigers sitting peacefully next to Panda bears and Indian elephants next to orang-

utans, some with spirit guides, some without.

Chapter Thirteen

The forest deer and the Grizzly bear pushed Sarah and Tom lightly, with their noses pressed against small of the children's backs, until the globe of light surrounding the animals enveloped Tom and Sarah, too.

Mother Nature called for silence. All the animals quietened down immediately, except for two baboons who chuckled noisily at something, until a huge Gnu coughed loudly enough for them to notice. Mother Nature approached the two baboons and ordered them to the back of the circle of animals, bringing shame down on all the primates.

A loud rumbling could be felt beneath everyone's feet. It got louder and the trees and bushes started to tremble. As every creature there turned to look, the earth in front of Mother Nature split and ripped open and upwards, white light spewing upwards and outwards, until it formed a huge ball of light.

Within the light, a man stood, wearing white robes. He had long white hair and a beard of white and gold. He didn't speak, but turned, slowly checking over each shoulder. Then he said to Mother Nature in a deep voice, "Are all the continents represented here today?" She answered, "They are, My Lord."

He then raised his arms, lightning cracked through the trees around them in flashes of blue and silver, and the old man announced, "Let the trial begin."

Tom was taken away by a group of bears. They surrounded him and told him he had to be very careful of all his answers to their many questions; some answers would add to their confusion, others would get him eaten!

Through deep forests and up rocky mountainsides, the group of bears surrounding Tom grew from the five at the edge of the trial to over a thousand as they approached the mouth of a huge cave in the grey rocky cliff-side.

The bears showed Tom how they foraged for food, some in the trees, some on the ground, some eating berries and some catching fresh salmon in the mountain rivers. The huge Grizzly followed Tom wherever they went, visiting large bears from America, Pandas in China and tiny bears from the island of Madagascar.

All were interlinked through their DNA, even if they were separated by vast expanses of oceans and rivers. They were the bear family. There hadn't been a trial of this kind for over forty years, Tom was told by an elderly female Panda.

They treated Tom as though he was a distinguished guest, offering him leaves and berries from their winter stock piles.

Tom was in awe of everything he saw and heard. He knew there was an important lesson in all he was being shown, but for the life of him, he couldn't figure out how this was part of the trial.

His mind wandered to Sarah and how she was faring. The huge Grizzly that was Tom's spirit guide, nudged Tom with his nose and said in a deep gravelly voice, "Sarah is fine, focus on your time here!"

Startled, Tom snapped himself back to where he was. Surrounded by bears of all shapes and sizes, adults and cubs, Tom moved through the cave, as a whole year in the life of a bear was shown to him in what must have been only an hour. He was shown how to dig out soft sweet tasting roots from beneath damp logs and how to get honey without being stung by hordes of angry bees.

A few of the bears walked past Tom, some jabbering to him in barely audible squeaky voices, and some voices as deep and gruff as the old Grizzly that followed him everywhere, or they pushed him around with the nose nudge to the lower back. A black bear mother with two cubs in tow, came to speak to Tom.

She grunted at the Grizzly and put her front paws out in front of her and lowered her head. Tom's spirit guide said, "This is Nanya, my mate, the two little ones are Visha and Vash, my cubs. It is unusual for a Grizzly to mate with a black bear, but we mate for life. Who knows what nature will throw in your path. You must expect the unexpected."

The huge female bear looked up at Tom and then nudged her two young ones up to Tom. They were shy at first, but then they stepped up to him, sniffed his clothes and from either side, they licked his face in unison. Turning, they tucked in behind their mother, as she led them to the back of the cave, away from Tom. Tom was a little surprised, but happy. The bears seemed to have accepted him.

Chapter Fourteen

Tom's spirit guide said, "My name is Neath. I will guide you as best as I can, but I have no understanding of the human ways. You destroy trees and dig up the earth to find tiny pieces of gold stone. Vast amounts of forest, where I was born in North America are now gone. Trees turned into furniture and hillsides full of human waste, plastic chairs and dolls in human form.

"We have no need of such things, we do not have armies to fight back, as we are pushed and hunted off land that has been bear land for thousands of years. I am not blaming you, Tom, but I must make you see what your kind have done. Humans are to blame for masses of destruction and slaughter, not only of the creatures of the forest, plains and oceans, but of each other in the name of greed and religion.

In Russia, China, Africa, Europe and the Arctic, bears have been hunted for their coats or for sport by men. You need to know the fear instilled in all animals of the smell and scent of man. I am happy that my family like you."

Tom saw Neath in a new light and understood now why he was his spirit guide. Tom hated the fact that councils would tear up a beautiful and ancient forest to build more and more car parks and shopping malls.

Neath, the bear

Neath

Tom had joined the protest that was being organised by adults in his neighbourhood against the diggers and builders of the council. Neath helped Tom see how nature was directly affected from the bear's point of view.

He saw huge amounts of forest destroyed and cities being built, trees uprooted then replanted to make a park within the city, or a fancy garden at a big house. Tom sat on an almost flat rock and stared out at the countryside before him. He saw no telegraph poles or overhead pylon wires on the horizon.

No white streaks across the sky from aircraft miles above the Earth's surface. All he saw was undisturbed nature, no roads, no buildings, just nature. He looked back at Neath and was about to ask, how this was possible, when Neath said in his deep rumbling voice, "This is not the 'Up'. This is the 'Down'. This is how we want it to stay. Your world is up there, ours is down here."

Tom wasn't sure how the creatures of the forest had possibly built a whole new world right under the humans' feet and that other than him and Sarah, no one knew about it. Lots went on down here that effected what happens in the 'Up'. His world was a selfish one. An eye for an eye and all that jazz, but this was perfect to him and he wished he could stay.

Chapter Fifteen

Sarah fell backwards and sideways as the buckles on her stool released her without notice. She fell into what felt like a bunch of tree branches, but as she tried to stand, she realised she was two metres off the ground. Turning in her branch-like seat, she saw she was sitting in the middle of a huge wrack of antlers.

Embarrassed, she tried to wiggle into a position to climb down, when a whispered voice called out to her, "Be still, child. Or we will both tumble forward." The huge male stag cantered away into the forest, with other deer falling into single file behind.

A cool stream ran through the forest, alongside which they ran, birds on the ground stepped off to one side to allow the stag and his load to pass. The pheasants were just about to continue pecking at the soil, when they realised the huge stag with a human on his antlers was not alone, they got spun in circles as deer after deer trotted past.

To Sarah, it was comical, the pheasants spun out of control, looking dizzy and ruffled. Sarah's spirit guide bounded on, while she hung on for dear life. The canter slowed to a trot.

Laid out before them was a beautiful clearing about twenty metres in diameter. The sun shone down in rays through the branches here and there, giving the stunning little clearing an almost majestical feeling. The huge forest deer slowly came to a halt. Graciously, it bowed forward, allowing Sarah to reach out with her feet and find firm ground once more.

She looked around in absolute wonder. To her left, a gentle waterfall flowed into a shallow pool of crisp, clear looking water, where fish of many colours swam or dived clear to snap at a passing fly. To her right, the grass was longer and seemed to fall downhill slightly as it re-joined the forest.

Here stood another huge forest deer with a huge wrack of glistening antlers, but the hair around his mouth was white and the tip of his right antler was broken off. Sarah felt her spirit guide nudge her in the back gently, until she stood less than a metre from this magnificent beast.

"Sarah Davidson, this is my father, White Socks, King of the higher plains." Sarah bowed gracefully to the beast, as he stared at her with his bloodshot, ancient looking eyes. The silence grew. Behind the old deer, young deer began to appear, forming ranks on both sides and seeming to pack out the forest that previously looked empty.

The silence was broken, as the old deer lifted its huge head and barked a long coughing rasp. Every muscle in his neck and shoulders tensed, as he said in a deep voice, "This human has been brought to us by Mother Nature herself. Transported by my son, Golden Eyes, Prince of the lower plains. Does any creature here today doubt my authority?"

White Socks, King of the Forest

Not a sound could be heard in the forest. Even the stream seemed to have stopped its splashing and tinkling sound. Sarah could hear her heart beating in her chest. The King spoke again. "Four does will guide and protect you here. Two of my wives and two of my daughters. They will teach you everything this forest and our history have to offer you. Golden Eyes will keep you safe, he will share his food and fresh water. For this trial, you are our guest and no creature shall challenge me or they suffer the consequences."

Chapter Sixteen

Four huge deer without antlers, but with big brown eyes and lighter fur came and stood either side of Sarah, until the glow from the light surrounding Golden Eyes engulfed them all. With small wet nudges in her back, Sarah was guided high up a hillside, where the forest thinned out and the air became cooler.

There were no mosquitoes here and the smells of the moss and the damp forest floor were gone, too.

"This is where every Deer's' journey in life begins. If the young cannot survive a season away from their mothers, they are abandoned. Here, the food is hard to find and the nights are cold. Many young work together as teams and go on to live fruitful lives; others are taken by hunters and never seen again. There are traps and snares here that will strangle the life out of a young inexperienced deer in a matter of hours.

"Our punishment may seem harsh, but we protect our families with our lives. Fires here are not started by the animals. It's your kind that brings danger and death to the creatures of the forest."

It started to rain. Sarah stood and looked around. It was a cold and miserable place. Nowhere to stand under a tree to keep out of the rain, but Sarah didn't feel the cold as she stood with animals either side of her. They weren't touching her, but she could feel the warmth of their bodies. She was beginning to learn of the secrets that were part of the Earth. Storms worse than any on the surface of our planet and more water than all the oceans.

Chapter Seventeen

The doe pushed these thoughts through Sarah's mind.

A mass of gas formed a hundred miles above our planet and gave us our atmosphere. Wrapping Earth in a protective blanket, without the atmosphere, there would be no life. Everything that happened in our world was governed from down here.

There's another force of nature inside the Earth that we take for granted. It's true that without the sun, we wouldn't be able to grow food, but the life that begins that food starts from beneath a crust almost forty-eight kilometres thick below the surface of our planet.

Volcanoes often spill out spores of the heated molten rock, but they are mere tiny holes like the sweat pores on our skin. Magma grows into enormous crystals that we collect, and we shake our heads in wonder at the energy from within the crystals. The Earth's crust is formed from seven large pieces, called plates, some pulling apart, others crashing together.

The Alps in Europe are proof of two large plates crashing together over fourteen million years ago. It's actually a part of Africa in the middle of Europe.

The Earth is always in motion. All the coal on Earth is the fossilised remains of an ancient forest.

All these images of growth and of an ancient Earth were being blasted through Sarah's eyes telepathically, as though she was watching a movie in the comfort of her own home. Humans have grown from unthinking creatures into the cause of pain and suffering for hundreds of thousands of creatures in the world above.

Chapter Eighteen

Sarah could see now why these animals didn't trust her instinctively. The old matriarch of the forest came strolling over to Sarah, as if they were old friends and said, "Our King wishes you to know lots more of information about deer and how our worlds work in unison. Kneel and grasp my head with both your hands, I'll be sleeping and telepathically you will gain information." Sarah could feel the rush of thoughts ripping through her mind, and she didn't struggle, she just let the information flow.

White-tailed deer have a wide range across various parts of North America. They can be found in southern Canadian provinces such as Alberta, Saskatchewan and British Columbia. White-tailed deer are also found throughout most of the United States, except for the most western states of California, Utah, Nevada or Alaska.

They are found in Mexico, Central America and even northern parts of South America. Recently, white-tailed deer have been introduced to Scandinavia. The habitat of the white-tailed deer is most often the temperate deciduous forests of the United States and southern Canada.

Another hunting horn could be heard far off in Sarah's dreaming mind. She stirred awake and saw the elderly female deer, who had given her these visions and facts had gone.

She waited patiently for what would happen next. Her spirit guide also waited quietly behind her, until she could stand the silence no longer and said, "Ok, I have learnt about forest creatures and how they are affected by the climate and loss of habitation all over the world, but I'm thirteen years old, how will what I do have any effect on the future?"

Mother Nature appeared through a cloud of gently falling leaves that shimmered and twisted as they fell.

She looked at Sarah and said, "There will be enough time for your questions, when you are older. I am the superior being down here and I think I have made a terrible mistake, I seriously think I must switch yours and Tom's spirit guides. I will bring him here now and we can get this transformation over with.

Tom was standing on a rocky plateau, looking out over the tree tops of a massive forest. A flash of blue light appeared off to his right and before he knew what was happening, one of the racing stools had whisked him off his feet. He never got a chance to say goodbye to any of the bears.

He thought to himself, he must try and concentrate on the bigger picture. The stool ran smoothly towards a solid rock cliff face.

Tom leaned back and tried to wriggle free. The stool ran on at a high speed. A strangled AAGGHHH sound escaped Tom's throat, as the rock face was parted just as if it was a curtain-like substance and Tom found himself in a wooded clearing with Sarah and Mother Nature. "Children, I have made a huge mistake." Tom and Sarah looked at each other. "I have had too much influence on your spirit guides, they will switch immediately."

An earth-shattering crash could be heard far off in the distance. A blue light appeared over the hill to the right and Tom's spirit guide was dragged to its knees in front of Mother Nature.

A screaming and crashing of branches followed as Sarah's spirit guide was also brought before the collector of souls. She told them through the power of telepathy that they would be swapping spirit guides as the deer and bear were too powerful for the individuals they had been drawn to, so they would switch and carry the knowledge with them from what they had already learnt and experienced. They wouldn't have to go off now and learn to be a new spirit guide and all the necessary animals linked to their guides; they would gain it all in an instant. Mother Nature sat the children down in a

grassy clearing near a rippling stream.

Chapter Nineteen

She addressed them both, "To understand everything in the 'Down' and the 'Up', you must learn how everything works. We will start with the seasons. Winter, spring, summer and autumn. They are four periods neatly cut into three months each, to cover the twelve months in a human's year. Not just a coincidence." "All has been carefully planned and thought out by beings much stronger and wiser than ourselves, but man has been led to believe it was all their own idea because God knows humans have an ego."

Winter gives plants and animals a chance to take a break from the replenishments it provides in the other nine months of the year. Three months doesn't seem to be an awfully long time, but for plants to recharge and filter out mistakes and evolve through a transitional period, forming growth within their heart and a new layer of bark on their outer shell.

A single tree may go through a hundred and fifty transitional periods in its life time. Evidence is seen, when a dead tree is cut down for fire wood or furniture and can be found within the rings. You will learn all life has to offer for every living creature before you can be allowed back to the 'Up' that will let you make decisions that will affect every creature up there and down here.

Winter is followed by spring. Flowers shake off their icy shackles and breathe new life into meadows and forest floors. Young animals take a lung full of oxygen for the first time and they have a lot to learn in a short period of time or they will not survive the winter. Bears come out of hibernation, hungry and weak. The rivers are bursting with fish.

The fallow deer are plump and ready to become a meal. Nothing is wasted. The seasons give new life to everything. From the smallest amoeba to the giant Grizzly bear. Everything needs oxygen. Everything needs water, air and food of some kind."

Mother Nature shifted her gaze and looked out over the rocky hilltops beyond the forest.

"Tom, Sarah, you are our future. Sarah, you will become a doctor. Tom, you will become a vet." Tom and Sarah looked at each other and burst into fits of laughter. Mother Nature let out a low angry growl that instinctively, the kids knew she was not happy with them laughing.

"You are early teens, 13 is a tender age, no longer a child and not an adult either. At that age, you just want to be older, but time will come to you both, you can be sure of that."

Mother Nature stood and told Tom and Sarah to follow her. She walked through the forest explaining things to them as they walked. The grass by the stream would only grow to a certain length for a reason. It would feed some animals as part of their diet or become a part of the bedding for smaller animals and birds to fill their nests. Bugs lived amongst the grass stems. Rodents and small animals would tuck into the grass; some would prefer the roots or the seeds and then the whole system would be recycled through the spoor of each creature. Tom sat wide eyed as a vixen with four cubs in tow, walked to the stream's edge and drank fully, whilst keeping one beady eye on her young and playful cubs. An owl hooted high up in the trees. The vixen froze to her spot and the cubs came close and crawled under her. Mother Nature stood still, while a hungry and dishevelled looking badger barged its way out from under some bushes.

"Good afternoon," Mother Nature said to the huge furry brute. Its eyes were pink and old looking. Its huge black head with the two distinctive white stripes down its face, turned slowly to face Mother Nature.

"Oh excuse me, Madam, I was sleeping. Then I heard a rumble through my sett and I couldn't get back to sleep, as I had a monstrous headache and a thirst. Pardon my language around your young 'uns. What's caused this ruckus?"

"We have had a meeting of the minds, Mr Badger. We have held a court for all creatures of the 'Below' to change the course of nature. Did you not get notification, Sir?"

The badger stood on its rear legs and scratched its behind against the protruding lower branches of a thorny tree and said, "Pardon again, Madam, no one tells old Piggy anything, I'll just dig for worms and then go back to sleep, nothing good comes of sticking one's snout into other people's business!"

Mother Nature turned and smiled at Tom and Sarah. She explained that although her business was to guard and protect every living creature, some creatures were more stubborn and stuck in their ways than others.

They continued on through the forest. Mother Nature stooped to pick up a brown leaf from the overgrown pathway in front of them and said, "This leaf may seem dead and of no use to anyone, but as the fine fibres crumble from the stem to join the other particles on the forest floor, some will be eaten and others will become another layer of the forest's blanket. Remember, nothing is wasted, everything has a use!"

This made Sarah think of the tons of rubbish at the land fill. Human waste had no use. What couldn't be recycled would be buried. Humans waste so much and use so little.

Tom felt like an honoured guest at a private party. Normally, he wouldn't go alone to the deeper darker parts of a forest, but today he felt sure he would see and experience things that were outside of his day-to-day routine. He had already seen creatures beyond his wildest imaginations and he was sharing them with his best friend in the whole world.

He looked back at Sarah, who was listening intently, as Mother Nature spoke of the fish in the stream. Her hair was golden.

Her huge blue eyes sparkled in the sunlight sprinkling through the treetop canopy and her nose was slightly red from a little sunburn.

Lost in thoughts of grandeur, Tom didn't see the young sapling in his path and walked straight into it. It slapped him in the face with a skinny leafy branch and Tom yelped as if he'd been stung by a bee. Both Mother Nature and Sarah burst out laughing and said, "Wake up, Tom!" He was a little embarrassed, but enjoyed their attention. He kept pace with the ladies, but kept just a little behind them, lost in thought. Tom stumbled again and looked shame-faced at the two ladies, who stopped to look back at their clumsy companion. "Are you already too tired of walking and learning?" Asked Mother Nature.

Tom stared at the floor and said, "It was all interesting in the beginning, but I'm rather bored now and could really use a nap, if we are going to be doing this the whole day." Mother Nature snapped her fingers and Tom fell instantly into a deep sleep. She took Sarah to one side and said to her, "Let's do this before his ego destroys you both and any plans of yours or of humanity's future.

"I must inform you that whatever plans you have in the future will always be intertwined with Tom." Sarah sat on her haunches and said softly, "I understand. Tom is stubborn sometimes, but he sees logic in a different way. He may not work things out in the normal way, but he somehow gets the right answer in the end." Mother Nature took hold of Sarah's hand and knelt down to put her hand on Tom's forehead.

She told Sarah she was giving them a soothing spell to calm their nerves, but she was also giving them photographic memories and the ability to learn and understand everything they were taught at school, college and university.

They were very fortunate, no more struggling with homework and assignments, but they had no idea of all of that yet.

Tom woke with a start. He was on his own bed. The dawn sun was creeping over the city. He yawned and sat up. Looking at his watch, he saw it was just before five in the morning. The small window on the dial of his wristwatch said SAT. Saturday, thought Tom.

A chance to meet up with Sarah and discuss the events that had taken place, would be a great way to start the weekend. He walked out of his bedroom and into the family bathroom.

Chapter Twenty

Sarah heard her Mother call out, "Sarah, breakfast is ready." She sat bolt upright in bed. Startled, she lifted the duvet and to her amazement, she realised she was in her pyjamas. My word, she thought, that was a weird dream. She swung into the bathroom to brush her teeth and wash her face.

Plenty of time to tidy up later. Now her tummy rumbled at the smell of frying eggs. Her Mother sat opposite her, looking over the brim of her tea cup with questioning eyes. "So, tell me what was so important that you missed a day at the mall and so tiring that you would go to bed without supper?"

Sarah didn't know where to begin, so she told her Mom that Tom and she were studying and listening to music.

Her Mom seemed satisfied with the answer and moved the subject onto curtains and redecorating the spare room. Sarah thought about everything that had happened and wondered to herself, what Tom would say at their two o'clock meeting at the cinema this afternoon.

End of Book One

Printed in Great Britain
by Amazon